FOURTH-GRADE FUSS

JOHANNA HURWITZ

FOURTH-GRADE FUSS

Illustrated by **ANDY HAMMOND**

SCHOLASTIC INC.
New York Toronto London Auckland
Sydney Mexico City New Delhi Hong Kong

ISBN: 978-0-545-22387-4

Text copyright © 2004 by Johanna Hurwitz.
Illustrations copyright © 2004 by Andy Hammond. All rights
reserved. Published by Scholastic Inc., 557 Broadway, New York,
NY 10012, by arrangement with HarperCollins Children's Books,
a division of HarperCollins Publishers. SCHOLASTIC and associ-
ated logos are trademarks and/or registered trademarks
of Scholastic Inc.

20   14/0

Printed in the U.S.A.   40

First Scholastic printing, December 2009

Typography by Nicole de las Heras

*For all the hardworking fourth graders and
their teachers throughout the country,
but especially for those students at C.E.S. 35
in the Bronx (formerly known as P.S. 35),
where I spent my elementary school years*

CONTENTS

1 · Welcome to Fourth Grade

Julio Sanchez was really glad to be in the same fourth-grade class as his pal Lucas Cott. Lucas was very smart and he was also very funny. It was impossible to sit in a classroom with Lucas and not double over with laughter at least once, or maybe even twice a day. Lucas always did or said something really crazy. As far as Julio was concerned, being in the same class as Lucas was funnier than any comedy program on TV.

One morning soon after the new school year began, Lucas realized he'd forgotten to do his homework. Instead of just admitting it and promising to be better prepared in the future, Lucas put on a whole show for the class.

He fell to the floor with a loud clatter. "I bumped my head," he moaned as he stood up. "Where am I? I think I have a concussion." He paused for a moment. "I also have amnesia."

"I doubt it," said their teacher, Mrs. Schraalenburgh. "Get in your seat and take out your homework," she told him.

Lucas looked around. "Which seat is mine?" he asked one of the girls who was sitting nearby.

Everyone started laughing because they knew Lucas was just pretending. And Julio watched his friend with amazement. He didn't know how Lucas managed to keep a straight face. Lucas would probably make a great actor when he grew up. He was a great actor already.

Mrs. Schraalenburgh came over and took Lucas by

the arm. She moved him toward his seat. "Does it look familiar?" she asked him.

"Where am I?" Lucas asked again. "Is this a school?"

"Not only is this a school," Mrs. Schraalenburgh told him, "but if you don't sit in your seat and behave, I'm afraid I'll have to send you down to the principal's office."

"To Mr. Herbertson?" asked Lucas, forgetting that he had amnesia.

"The very one," said the teacher.

No one wanted to be sent to the principal's office. Not even Lucas. But for the rest of the morning, Julio grinned whenever he thought of his friend pretending not to know where he was.

On the following Saturday, Julio went with Lucas to see a World War II film at the local movie house. When the picture was over and they left the theater, Lucas spoke with a phony German accent as the boys walked home. It sounded hilarious to Julio. But it was even funnier when Lucas answered questions in his newly acquired German accent on Monday morning at school.

At first Mrs. Schraalenburgh tried to ignore

Lucas's behavior. But finally she said to him, "Lucas, did you have sauerbraten for dinner last night?"

"Vas is dat? Zauerbraten?" Lucas asked in his imitation German voice.

"That is what you'll find out and write a report on for tomorrow," the teacher responded. To help him, she wrote the word on the chalkboard.

And so on Tuesday, Lucas came to school with an extra homework assignment.

Cricket Kaufman was in their class too. Julio had been in classes with Cricket since he moved to town when he was in second grade. Cricket was perfect, which was bad enough. But to make matters worse, Cricket knew she was perfect and showed off a lot. When Lucas got the extra sauerbraten assignment, Cricket brought in a recipe for the dish the next day. That's how everyone in the class learned that it was a traditional German meal, sort of like pot roast. Only according to Cricket's recipe, the gravy was made of sour cream and ground gingersnap cookies. It sounded odd and made everyone laugh. But Julio would have been willing to try it if it was ever served for lunch in the school cafeteria. Anyhow, it was just like Cricket to do Lucas's homework and to do it better than he did.

Still, now that they were in fourth grade, both Lucas and Cricket began to change. Lucas clowned around a bit less. And Cricket began to act differently too. She gradually seemed more like a human being and not a perfectly programmed robot student who did everything better than everyone else.

Julio liked Mrs. Schraalenburgh, his fourth-grade teacher. The name was a mouthful and the spelling was worse. There was a school rumor that only the brightest students were put into Mrs. Schraalenburgh's class each year. Who else would be able to say and spell that difficult name? So when Julio had first discovered that he was in her section of fourth grade, he worried that a mistake had been made. No one would ever say that Julio was one of the smarter students in his grade.

Everyone knew that this was the year that all the students took the statewide standardized tests in math and language skills. When they were younger, fourth grade seemed so far away. Julio and his friends had tiptoed past the fourth-grade classrooms each spring and looked in awe at the signs posted on the doors:

QUIET PLEASE.
. . .
TEST IN PROGRESS.

And they had felt a great relief that they were not sitting behind those closed doors, chewing on pencils while they racked their brains for the correct answers.

Once during the summer between third and fourth grade, when Lucas and Julio were playing together, Lucas had mentioned the forthcoming tests. "My mom says not to worry about them," Lucas had told his friend. "She says I'll do just fine."

Julio's mom never talked about the tests at all. She probably didn't know they existed. When Julio's older brothers, Ramon and Nelson, were in fourth grade, the family hadn't lived in this community, not even in this state. Nowadays Mrs. Sanchez was head chambermaid at Sycamore

Shade Motor Inn. Even though she had to work hard doing her own duties and supervising the other chambermaids, it was the best-paying job she'd ever had, so she was very pleased. Since Julio's father was no longer alive, his mother had to support the family. Mrs. Sanchez left the house early in the morning and came home in time for supper. By then she'd be exhausted. Sometimes Julio's grandmother, who lived with them, prepared the evening meal. His grandmother spoke Spanish and didn't know more than a dozen words of English, but she was a pretty good cook. Other days, if their grandmother's arthritis was acting up, Julio, Ramon, and Nelson put the meal together. Nothing special: hamburgers or a pot of spaghetti with sauce out of a jar or some other easy-to-prepare thing. Mrs. Sanchez always asked her sons about school, but she'd been born in Puerto Rico and didn't always understand all the things that were going on here. So Julio had never discussed the standardized tests for fourth graders with her. Besides, it was still a long way off until April. He wasn't going to think about it now.

7

Before many days of the new school year had passed, Cricket gathered her classmates around her. "I was talking to Nancy Ross, who's in Mrs. Lento's class. She says they're busy doing work to get ready for the big tests. But we haven't done anything at all yet. Do you realize we won't be prepared?" she said with alarm.

"Hey, Cricket. You're so smart you could take the tests this afternoon and you'd do great," Julio told her.

"Do you really think so?" asked Cricket, beaming at her classmate.

"Yep."

"Well, I still think we should be doing practice tests and things like the other fourth graders. You can't be too prepared for the big tests. Besides, I want to score in the top percentile."

Julio didn't even know what that meant.

"If you want to be prepared, join the Boy Scouts," Lucas said. "That's their motto. *Be prepared*."

"Very funny," said Cricket, scowling at Lucas.

"Anyhow, I'm glad we're not talking about those tests in our class. I don't want to think about them," said Lucas.

That's the way Julio felt too. He just wished that his head was as smart as Cricket's and Lucas's. But there was no fooling himself. He might be in Mrs. Schraalenburgh's class. He had even learned how to spell her name. But he didn't know how he'd manage the tests. And he didn't know what would happen if he really goofed up. He shuddered just thinking about it.

"Someone just walked over your grave," Cricket told him.

"What are you talking about?" Julio asked her.

"I saw you give a shiver. That's what my great-aunt always says if she shivers. Someone walked over her grave."

"You're crazy," said Julio. But secretly he had something else to worry about. Would these tests be the end of him? Could you die from taking the big tests?

2 · Tests, Tests, Tests

When October came and Mrs. Schraalenburgh still hadn't mentioned the statewide tests, Cricket grew more concerned than ever. Finally she raised the question. "How come all the other fourth-grade classes are studying for the big standardized tests and we're not?" she asked their teacher.

"The tests that you're referring to won't be given

until April," Mrs. Schraalenburgh replied. "I don't want to spend all our class time getting ready for them. There are many things that one needs to learn when one is in fourth grade in addition to the information covered on the state exam."

"But how can we do as well as the other kids, then?" asked Cricket.

Julio knew Cricket's goal was not to do as well as other kids. She wanted to do *better* than them.

"I promise you that this is not something you have to worry about," the teacher said.

Julio wondered what she meant. The word *you* could apply to the whole class or it could just mean Cricket.

"But why are the other classes doing different work from us?" Cricket asked. She was like a dog with a bone, thought Julio. She would not give it up.

"Listen, class," Mrs. Schraalenburgh said, looking around the room to be certain that she had everyone's attention before her eyes returned to Cricket's face. "The standardized tests that you will be taking in April are given to every single fourth grader in this state. They're given so we can measure how students are doing compared to other fourth graders in this school, and in all the other schools within the state." Mrs. Schraalenburgh paused for a moment. "But did you know that these statewide tests are given to check the teachers as much as the students? If my classes always did poorly on the tests, I wouldn't be standing in front of this room. The truth is, my students do just as well as, or perhaps even better than, the other fourth graders throughout the state. And my method is not to do anything about the tests before we return to school in January after the New Year. Trust me. You'll be prepared for those big tests. And in the meantime, let's not make a fuss about them." She waited a moment for this information to sink in. "Can you be patient?" she asked Cricket.

"I guess so," Cricket said reluctantly, because she was still not totally convinced.

"I can be patient even though I'm not in a hospital," said a voice. Lucas had been practicing ventriloquism from a book he'd gotten at the library. But either the book wasn't very good or else Lucas hadn't mastered the skill yet, because everyone knew who said those words. And everyone laughed.

"Take care of yourself. I don't want you in the hospital," Mrs. Schraalenburgh said. She looked directly at Lucas, though she didn't mention his name. Obviously she'd known who had made that joke too, Julio thought. Lucas would have to work at throwing his voice a whole lot more if he wanted to fool their teacher.

It was weird. Just as the students began talking about tests at school, there was a lot of discussion about tests at Julio's home, too. Lately his grandmother hadn't been feeling very well. She was tired all the time, and she complained that everything hurt her— her eyes, her head, her legs, her feet, and her stomach, too. "I have too much body," she moaned to the family. Mrs. Sanchez was worried about her mother, and so she arranged to take time off from work. She spent two days at the local medical center while her mother took a battery of tests to check her health. On the second day, when they returned home, Julio's grandmother turned to her daughter and said, "I'm going to bed."

"It's only four o'clock," said Julio, who had just come home from school a short while before.

"It's four o'clock for you," said his grandmother in Spanish. "For me it's four hundred o'clock. I'm exhausted."

Julio turned to his mother for an explanation.

"Your grandmother has had a lot of tests," she said. "It's worn her out."

"Tests?" asked Julio. His grandmother hardly knew any English. He couldn't imagine how in the world she could be tested. Maybe they had special tests in Spanish for people like her.

But then Mrs. Sanchez went on to explain. "She had a blood test and a test to check if her heart is working properly and a lot of other medical procedures. It's not easy getting old," she warned her sons. "But maybe there are some medicines to help her. The doctor doesn't want to prescribe a new and stronger arthritis medication until he's certain that it won't have a bad effect on other parts of her body.

And he wants to be sure that nothing else is wrong with her too."

"Poor Abuela," said Julio.

As if statewide school tests and medical tests weren't enough, Ramon had a test on the brain too.

Ramon was a high school senior and he was taking driver's ed. He had learned all the rules about driving, and now he was actually going out in a car twice a week with an instructor and two other students. Each student had a chance to drive the school-owned car and practice making right and left turns. Then they progressed to U-turns and parallel parking. Ramon loved driving. For two years now he'd been saving money from his after-school jobs to buy a car. "It won't be a new car, of course," he explained to Julio. "New cars cost thousands and thousands of dollars. But by the time I get my driver's license, I should have about two thousand dollars in the bank. And I can get somebody's old car with that money."

"Don't forget, you need money for insurance and for gas," their mother reminded Ramon. "If you're not careful, that car will own you instead of the other way around. You don't want to spend every penny you ever earn maintaining a car."

"I won't care," said Ramon, grinning broadly. "You know I've wanted a car since I was a little kid."

"That's true enough," Mrs. Sanchez agreed, nodding.

Their grandmother, who had come back into the room, made a comment in Spanish. "He was pushing a slice of bread along the table and making sounds like a car when he was two years old."

Nelson let out a loud laugh. "Well, if you don't buy a car, you can get an awful lot of bread for two thousand dollars," he told Ramon. "White bread, whole wheat bread, rye bread, rolls. Rolls would be the best for pushing across the table. *Veroom, veroom*," he said, trying to imitate a car speeding off. Nelson was two years younger than Ramon, so he still had a long wait until he could think about owning a car.

Ramon looked at Nelson and shrugged. "I can't get a car until I get my license," he reminded his family. "And I can't get a license until I pass my driving test. It's not going to be easy."

"It will be a piece of cake for you," said Julio to

his brother. He looked up to his older brother and couldn't imagine Ramon not succeeding in everything he did.

"No. It will be a slice of bread," said Nelson.

"You won't be taking the test for another couple of months," Mrs. Sanchez said. "By then you'll be able to drive fine. You'll know how to make those turns perfectly."

"You can make a you-turn," said Julio, trying to make a joke.

"Yeah, well, here's my problem," said Ramon. "I'm the only one in driver's ed whose family doesn't own a car. Everyone else gets extra practice by going driving with their parents. But the only time I'm behind the wheel is the fifteen or so minutes of class time. It's just not enough. And I wish I didn't have to take a road test. Why can't you finish taking your driving lessons and then begin driving? The way you take freshman English in high school and then automatically go on to sophomore and junior and senior English?"

"You have tests in school all the time," Mrs. Sanchez pointed out.

"But driving is different. If you couldn't drive, you wouldn't drive."

"No way," said Nelson. "There are enough bad drivers out on the roads now who did pass tests. Imagine if anyone who thought they were good enough just got behind the wheel of a car. You'd be in danger every time you crossed the street."

"You're absolutely right," Mrs. Sanchez said to Nelson. Then she turned to Ramon. "Once you have your license, you'll be glad you can be sure the other drivers on the road have passed their driving tests, too."

"Yeah. Well, I sure wish we owned a car so I could practice more," Ramon said.

"Don't worry," Julio told his brother. "You're so smart, you won't need as much time as everyone else to learn how to drive." Julio looked proudly at his older brother. He just knew Ramon was clever enough to do anything he wanted to.

3 · The Garage Sale

On a Saturday in mid-October, Lucas Cott's parents held a garage sale. When school was out on the day before the sale, Julio helped Lucás post signs on trees and telephone poles in the neighborhood. The signs had been created by Mrs. Cott on the family's computer. They said:

BIG, BIG, BIG Sale
Books, Toys, Clothes, Dishes,
Bric-a-brac, etc.
• • •
Saturday, October 15
10 A.M.–4 P.M.
74 Ridge Road

Julio enjoyed putting up the signs, and he took it for granted that this was just the beginning. Of course he was going to help out at the sale.

"I've got a job today too," Julio announced proudly as Nelson and Ramon were getting ready to leave for their part-time work the next morning.

"No kidding?" asked Ramon as he zipped his jacket.

"I'm going over to help Lucas help his parents," Julio explained. "They're having a garage sale."

"Have fun," Nelson called to him as he followed Ramon out the door.

"I know the garage sale will be great," Julio told his mother and grandmother, who were still sitting at the table drinking their morning coffee. "Remember that time when I was only in second grade? Ramon and I were walking down the street and we passed a garage sale? He bought me a baseball mitt for only a quarter. I still have it."

"They're lucky the weather is so good," commented Mrs. Sanchez as she buttered a slice of toast.

"Garage sale?" asked Julio's grandmother. "How much does it cost? One of these days when Ramon gets a car he's going to need a garage for it."

Julio swallowed the cornflakes in his mouth so he could explain to her. "They're not selling their garage," he said, laughing. "A garage sale means that they're selling all the junk that they've been keeping in their garage or basement. It's all stuff they want to get rid of, and if they're lucky people will buy it from them."

"Too bad," said Julio's grandmother. "I would like to buy a garage for Ramon as a surprise."

"It would be a very big surprise since he doesn't

have a car," said Julio.

"He doesn't even have his driver's license," added Mrs. Sanchez. "But don't worry. When the time comes and he has the license and a car, he can park out on the street."

"You're right," Julio's grandmother agreed. "But everyone likes a bargain. And I didn't understand. I thought this was one."

"That's the whole secret of garage sales," said Julio, spooning up the last of the milk in his cereal bowl. "People come to the sales looking for bargains. Lucas explained it all to me yesterday. They're hoping a lot of people will come and buy their stuff."

"Will you be home for lunch?" asked Mrs. Sanchez as Julio put his dish in the sink.

"Oh, no. The sale runs until four o'clock. So I won't be home until suppertime." Julio grabbed his jacket and planted quick kisses on his mother's and grandmother's foreheads. "See you then," he told them.

Although it wasn't yet nine o'clock when Julio arrived at Lucas's house, there was already lots of activity. But looking around, Julio was disappointed. Although Lucas and his father had brought both the kitchen and the dining-room tables outside and covered them with items for sale, there was no way that Julio would have described the sale as big, big, big. He wouldn't even call it big, big. It looked exactly like it was: two tables loaded with junk that the Cott family didn't want anymore.

Mrs. Cott was busy arranging her old set of dishes and some odd serving bowls on one of the tables. She put small price stickers on each article. "Hi, Julio," she called to him. "It's nice of you to come and help us."

"No sweat," Julio responded as he looked about.

Mr. Cott came outside carrying a pair of coffee tables for sale. They were quickly used to display items as well. There were several vases, a planter, and an old table lamp.

"You're just in time, Julio," Mr. Cott called out. "We need all the hands we can get."

Julio followed Mr. Cott inside the house, where a baby-sitter was entertaining Lucas's twin brothers, Marcus and Marius. Since the Cott family had to pay the baby-sitter, they might end up spending more money today than they made, Julio thought. He wondered if their baby-sitter could tell the boys apart. No matter how hard he tried, Julio always found it impossible to be certain which of Lucas's brothers was Marcus and which was Marius.

"You and Lucas can take these boxes outside," said Mr. Cott, pointing to some cartons. "I have to get the stuff up from the basement. There's still more junk— I mean sale items—down there."

Julio was curious to see what else the Cotts were selling. He had two dollars in his pocket and hoped that maybe he could find something to put away for a Christmas gift for someone in his family.

The first carton he took outside was filled with paperback books. They were mostly science-fiction titles. Julio thought that Nelson might like one, and so he selected the book with the most interesting picture on the cover. "How much are these books?" he called out to Mrs. Cott.

"Twenty-five cents apiece or five for a dollar" was the reply.

"Okay, I'm buying this one," said Julio, holding up the book he'd picked out.

"For you it's free," Mrs. Cott responded as she leaned an old vacuum cleaner against the dining-room table and placed a sticker on it.

"Wow, thanks," said Julio. He put the book in his jacket pocket and peeked into a second box, which Lucas had just set down. It contained copies of old *National Geographic* magazines. The boys made two piles of them on the dining-room table and then put the empty cartons underneath.

Marcus and Marius came running out of the house, followed by their baby-sitter. Each boy had several stuffed toys in his arms.

"Are you selling your teddy bears?" Julio asked them.

"These are baby toys," said one of the boys.

"We play with trucks now," said the other.

Lucas and Julio took the toys and arranged them on a tablecloth that Mrs. Cott had spread out on the ground.

One of the twins sat down on the cloth. "Don't sit there," said Julio. "Someone will think you're for sale."

Either Marcus or Marius jumped up. "No, I'm not. No one can buy me," he said.

"He's only joking," said Mrs. Cott, giving her son a hug as she pasted stickers on the teddy bears.

"Let's go back inside the house," the baby-sitter called to the twins. "We're going to do some finger painting."

"Finger painting. That's nice and messy," one of the brothers responded gleefully.

"Nice and messy," his twin echoed.

Julio was glad that his job was not taking care of Marcus and Marius. It would be hard work, and although he liked Lucas's little brothers, he didn't feel like spending his time cleaning them, and probably much of the house, too, after the finger painting was over.

"How much is that coffeepot?" a voice asked. Julio turned around. A woman was pointing to an electric percolator that Mrs. Cott had placed on the table.

"It's four dollars," said Julio, "but I don't think you can buy it yet. The sale doesn't open until ten o'clock."

"Don't be silly," said the woman. "I'll give you

three dollars for it."

"Just a minute," said Julio, running toward the house in search of one of Lucas's parents, who had both gone inside. "Let me find out."

He found Mrs. Cott, who was giving some instructions to the baby-sitter. "Can I sell your coffeepot for three dollars?" he asked her.

"You found a customer already?" asked Lucas's mother with surprise.

"Yep," said Julio proudly, although he hadn't done a thing but stand there.

"The pot is marked four dollars. Can she have it for less?"

"The prices are all negotiable. Let's get the most we can. But at the end of the day I really don't want to be left with all this stuff. So selling is the most important thing."

"Okay," said Julio. He rushed back to the potential customer. "You can have the coffeepot for three and a half dollars," he told the woman. He was prepared to reduce the pot further, but this was how he'd seen it done on TV.

"I don't know if it's worth that much," the woman said.

Julio shrugged his shoulders and counted silently to himself. He figured he'd count to ten before reducing the price. At seven, the woman opened her purse and pulled out three dollar bills and five dimes.

"Enjoy your coffee," shouted Julio as the woman went off.

"Where should I put the money?" Julio asked Lucas and his father, who were coming out of the house lugging old suitcases.

"You made money already?" asked Lucas, looking at his wristwatch. "Wow. Maybe we shouldn't sell these cases. Maybe we'll need them to put all the money in."

Mr. Cott took the money from Julio. "I'm going to sit over here." He pointed to a chair nearby. "Anyone who wants to buy something should be sent over to me. I'll be able to take their money and make change if necessary."

"Where do you want me to stay?" asked Julio.

"You're doing fine right where you are," Mr. Cott told him.

By ten o'clock there were several people strolling around in the Cotts' yard. People picked up things, turned them around, and put them back down again. But no sooner did someone put something down than someone else would pick it up. And some of those people actually bought the old dishes, the books, the suitcases, and the vacuum cleaner.

"Hey, look who's here," Julio called out to Lucas.

Cricket Kaufman was walking with her mother, who was pushing Cricket's little sister in a stroller.

"Hi, Cricket," Lucas called out. "Your sock's untied."

Cricket looked down at her feet.

"Ha, ha. I made you look. Socks don't have laces on them," Lucas shouted jubilantly.

Julio felt a little sorry for Cricket. Lucas always seemed to get the better of her, and today she wasn't even wearing shoes with laces. But she had fallen for Lucas's joke.

"You think you're so smart, don't you?" said Cricket.

"Yep," Lucas agreed with her. "That's because I am."

Cricket turned away from the boys and caught up with her mother. Mrs. Kaufman was standing near

Marcus and Marius's collection of stuffed toys and examining them. Julio watched as she selected one and held it out to Cricket's sister.

"Well, I think your family made another sale," said Julio as Mrs. Kaufman pushed the carriage over to where Mr. Cott was sitting and collecting money.

As lunchtime neared, Mrs. Cott came over to the boys. Her face was flushed from the morning's activity. "I'm going to phone and have a large pizza delivered for lunch," she told them. "Is that okay?"

"Super," said Julio.

"Get extra cheese," Lucas called after his mother. Then he added, "Get a big bottle of soda, too."

"You forgot to say *please*," Julio pointed out to his friend. But Mrs. Cott was already speaking on her cell phone and didn't seem to notice.

Julio convinced a man to buy a whole stack of the paperbacks. And he was just in the midst of flipping the pages of a *National Geographic*, in the hopes of arousing some interest in them, when the pizza arrived. By now enough items had sold that there was room on the table for the large box. Lucas opened it and steam arose together with the aroma of melted cheese and tomato sauce.

"Oh, I want a piece," a little boy called out to his mother.

"How much is the pizza?" the mother asked.

Julio was about to say it wasn't for sale when he caught Lucas's eye. "It's a dollar and a half for a slice," he said. "And it isn't secondhand. It's genuine new, never before eaten."

The woman smiled and paid for two slices.

"Oh, how clever," said another woman. "I don't know why more people don't sell food at their garage sales. Please give me a slice too," she said. "And I'll take a cup of that soda."

By the time Mrs. Cott came looking for a slice of the pizza, it was all gone. "I can't believe how fast that went!" she exclaimed, looking at the empty box. "Your father and I are hungry too," she said to her son.

"I'm still hungry," Lucas responded, without explaining that he hadn't eaten even a bite of the pizza.

"Then you'll have to settle for a peanut butter and

jelly sandwich. And you'll have to make it for yourself," his mother told him. "That's what your father
and I will be eating."

"Are you going to keep that money?" Julio asked
his friend.

"Well, later I'm going to tell my parents what we
did. But I bet they let me keep it."

"Then you better make me a peanut butter and
jelly sandwich before I collapse from starvation,"
Julio said. "A couple of those slices that we sold were
my lunch too."

"No problem," Lucas responded. "Keep an eye on
the table and I'll go fix them right now. What do you
like best—strawberry jam or grape jelly?"

The garage sale was a big success. Even after the
money for the baby-sitter and the pizza, Lucas's parents made eighty-seven dollars.

"And now we have lots more space to put things
that we buy at someone else's sale," said Mrs. Cott.

Julio walked home with the science-fiction paperback in one jacket pocket and a shopping bag hold-

ing an almost new blue woolen bathrobe that had once belonged to Mrs. Cott, which Julio thought would make a great gift for his mother at Christmas. Mr. Cott had refused to take any money from him for the robe. In his pocket were five dollars: the two dollars that he'd had in his pocket when he left the house in the morning and three additional dollars that Mrs. Cott made Lucas give him from the sale of the pizza slices he didn't get to eat. It had been a big, big, big sale after all.

4 · December Break

Even though school might not be Julio's favorite place in the world, he had to admit the days passed quickly. Before he knew it, Halloween and then Thanksgiving had come and gone. The days got shorter and colder, and all the local stores sported Christmas decorations. Christmas and the new year were approaching, and with them came a ten-day vacation from school.

On the next to the last day before the break, Zoe Mitchell, who was still called "the new girl" by all the students even though she'd moved to town in August and been in their class for four months, handed out invitations to every single student in Mrs. Schraalenburgh's class.

**PLEASE JOIN ME
AT THE LAKESIDE SKATING RINK**
17 Lakeshore Drive
On Thursday, December 27, at 10:30 A.M.
For skating, lunch, & fun.

If you've never skated before, this is a chance to learn.
Skates will be provided for anyone who doesn't own a pair.

There was a buzz throughout the class. Four of Julio's classmates were going out of town over the vacation. They looked disappointed that they would miss this special event. It was unusual for anyone to give a party for the entire class.

"I love to ice-skate," said Cricket proudly. "I'm pretty good at it too. Now you'll get to see me."

"Are you going to try out for the Olympics?" asked Lucas.

"How can I?" Cricket snapped back at him. "You know I'm planning to go to law school and eventually become the first woman president of the United States. Professional athletes spend hours every day practicing. I can't afford to use my time that way. But that doesn't mean I can't skate for fun."

"Yes, Madam President. You're right," said Lucas, teasing Cricket. She was the only person Julio or Lucas knew who had planned out her whole life far into the future.

"Cricket probably knows what she's having for supper when she's seventy-five years old," Lucas once told Julio. And Julio thought Lucas was right about that.

"I've never been skating," Julio admitted. "Is it hard?"

"If you've never skated, then you'll probably fall a hundred times," Cricket told him. "I almost never fall anymore," she bragged.

"Skating isn't so hard," Lucas told Julio. "It's the ice that's hard."

Julio wasn't afraid of falling. And he wasn't afraid of making a fool of himself at the skating rink. Parties were fun. An ice-skating party had to be fun and a challenge too. He was glad that Zoe had arranged to have ice skates for those without them.

On the morning of the party, Lucas's mother picked up Julio in her car. Lucas was in the back between the car seats holding Marcus and Marius. Julio squeezed into the small space near the door behind the driver. He wished there wasn't a law about kids sitting in the front seat. He was really squished.

"Hi, guys," he said to Lucas and his brothers.

"I want to ice-skate too," said either Marcus or Marius.

"Me too," said the other.

"You'll go ice-skating when you get bigger," their mother promised them.

"Tomorrow?" asked one of the twins.

"Not tomorrow. Another day."

"If I eat everything on my plate for lunch, I'll be bigger tomorrow," said Marcus or Marius.

"I'll eat everything too," said the other.

"But not big enough," replied their mother.

"Hey, guys. How old are you now, anyway?" asked Julio, although he knew the answer.

"Three," they both answered, holding out their fingers to show Julio the correct number.

"Well, I'm almost ten," said Julio. He held up both hands and wiggled all his fingers.

"This is going to be the very first time that I'm going ice-skating."

"That's too many fingers to wait," complained one of the twins.

"Maybe when you're four," Lucas's mother told the boys. "And if Julio learns how to skate, he can come and help Lucas and me watch over two boys going in two different directions. How about it, Julio?"

"Sure," said Julio. "I'll do all my falling today."

Lucas looked at Julio. "You should have put a

pillow inside your pants," he told his friend. "That ice is hard."

"Not as hard as math," said Julio, grinning. He may never have gone skating before, but Julio was a natural athlete and he'd never participated in any sport that he hadn't mastered.

"Have a good time," Lucas's mother called to the two older boys when they reached the skating rink.

"We will," Julio called back. It felt good to get out of the car and stretch his legs.

He followed Lucas up the steps. It was fun to see so many of his classmates sitting on wooden benches and lacing up ice skates. There were other, older kids too. They were classmates of Zoe's older sister, Halley. And of course, there were lots of people who came to skate who weren't part of the party group. It was a public rink and open to anyone who paid the admission fee.

Julio walked over to Zoe. "I don't have any skates," he told her.

"No problem," Zoe said. She led Julio over to an area where skates could be rented. The good thing was that Julio didn't have to pay for renting skates, just as he hadn't needed to pay the admission price either. It was all included in the party. The man asked Julio his shoe size and returned with a pair of black ice skates.

"Lace them up tight," the man instructed Julio.

"Okay," Julio agreed. He was eager to put on the skates and to try them out on the ice.

Lucas waited for Julio. "It always looks so easy when you see someone who can skate well," Lucas said. "But ice is slippery. And it's hard to keep your balance. I like sports where you wear sneakers better."

"Well, you can always look forward to lunch," Julio said. "And besides, wouldn't you have been disappointed if Zoe had only invited people who loved ice-skating and didn't include us?"

"I suppose," said Lucas.

Julio stood up. "So far, so good," he said as he followed Lucas toward the ice.

As they went on the ice, each of the party guests was given a red-and-black-striped woolen cap to wear. "This way we can keep track of everyone," Zoe explained to the boys.

Julio put on the cap. "It looks like we're a team," he said. "But you must have spent an awful lot of money."

"They were overstock at a company where my aunt is the accountant," Zoe reported. "She got them for free and the company was glad to get rid of them."

"Do we keep them?" asked Julio.

"You better," said Zoe. "Because I don't know what we would do at my house with fifty red-and-black woolen caps."

There were probably a hundred people on the ice, and half of them were wearing red-and-black caps. It really looked neat, Julio thought, as he stepped gingerly down on the ice. Almost at once, someone bumped into him and he lost his balance. His feet went out from under him and he landed on the ice with a thud.

"That's one," called out Lucas. "I wonder how many more times you'll fall before it's lunchtime?"

The rink was in the shape of a large oval. It took

Julio ten minutes to make his way around it, and during that time he fell once more.

Zoe had said they'd stop for lunch at noon. Julio looked at a large clock that was overhead. Fifty minutes to go. If he fell on the ice twice every ten minutes, he could expect to land on his behind another two times five, or on ten more occasions. He rubbed the seat of his pants and started his second round.

"Isn't this fun?" called Cricket.

Actually, it was. Before long Julio had caught the hang of skating and was doing very well. He didn't fall the estimated ten times. In fact, he made it all around the rink without falling. Then he was startled to see a familiar adult skating by wearing a red-and-black cap. While he stood gaping at the unexpected sight of his fourth-grade teacher on ice, Julio lost his balance and fell again. Imagine, even Mrs. Schraalenburgh had been invited to this party. And it looked like she was a pretty good skater, too.

"That's two!" shouted Lucas as he passed.

"No, it's three! What are you doing? Standing around and counting my falls?" Julio called back. He really didn't mind the falls. He was having a good time. Maybe he could convince his brothers to come ice-skating with him one of these days. By lunchtime, Julio had fallen just four times and had mastered the basics. He could glide along and he could stop. It had been great fun, but still, he was glad to take off the skates and go have something to eat.

Mrs. Schraalenburgh didn't stay for lunch. But the younger guests sat on long picnic-style tables and had hot dogs and French fries. It was a great party and a highlight of the holiday break from school.

5 · Five Pounds of Sugar

"All good things must come to an end," said Mrs. Sanchez on January third as her sons ate their breakfast.

"That's a very negative way of looking at things," said Nelson. But it was certainly true about the school vacation. It was time for all three Sanchez boys to return to their studies.

And in Mrs. Schraalenburgh's fourth grade, it

was time to begin preparation for the statewide exams. Only Cricket looked happy when their teacher handed out a sheet of problems that looked unfamiliar. As for Julio, he suddenly felt a twinge in his gut.

The page that the students were given was made up of ten math questions, but there were an awful lot of words involved too. You'd think it was a test of reading and not of math.

"Read each question through completely before you try to answer it," the teacher said.

Julio started reading.

1. A fisherman catches a trout that is twenty-eight inches long. In his refrigerator at home there is a lobster that is two feet long. Which is bigger, the trout or the lobster?

   a) lobster
   b) trout
   c) They are both the same.
   d) Don't have enough information to tell.

Julio started thinking. He was certain that there had never been a lobster in his refrigerator at home. And he was almost certain they'd never had trout at his house either. He wondered what trout tasted like. He thought about what it felt like to be a fish caught and pulled out of the water. Somewhere he'd heard that lobsters were thrown into a pot alive and boiled to death. He didn't think he'd ever want to eat a creature that was killed under those circumstances. He shuddered and quickly moved on to the next question.

2. How many ounces are there in a five-pound bag of sugar?

a) 20

b) 50

c) 80

d) none of the above

The reference to the five-pound bag of sugar immediately made Julio think of his grandmother. One of the results of her medical examination was the discovery that she was pre-diabetic. Julio had been very alarmed when he heard the news. *Diabetic* sounded like it had something to do with dying. He was relieved when his mother explained that it concerned the sugar in his grandmother's system and how her body used it. For the time being she wasn't taking any special medication, but she had been told to greatly reduce the amount of sugar and sweets that she consumed. In the past Julio's grandmother had always put three teaspoons of sugar into her coffee in the morning. Now she was using an artificial sweetener.

More important, Ramon was told not to bring home any more donuts. Julio's oldest brother worked at a donut shop. He received the minimum wage— and all the leftover donuts he wanted. Sometimes he would bring home a dozen day-old jelly donuts or custard cremes. Now, although their grandmother was the only one who had been forbidden to eat sweets, their mother felt it would be unfair to have the donuts in the house to tempt her.

"They really aren't good for any of us," Mrs.

Sanchez told her boys. Well, Ramon could eat some at work if he wanted, but Julio felt deprived. He missed the bag of donuts that had been sitting on the counter when he came home from school every day. Now, reading the problem in front of him, Julio thought about those donuts. Then, although it wasn't part of the problem, he wondered how many teaspoons were in a five-pound bag of sugar. He could imagine his grandmother happily spooning them into her coffee. She said she didn't like the aftertaste of the artificial sweetener. Sugar was better.

Around him, Julio began to hear a shuffling of paper and scraping of feet. Someone dropped a pencil on the floor and someone else sneezed. He looked up and saw that many of his classmates seemed to have finished the questions. Now they were waiting restlessly for the slowpokes like him. He felt that twinge in his gut again and sighed. Another of his grandmother's problems was that she had developed a nervous stomach. As he sat looking at the test paper before him, Julio decided he must have the same problem. His stomach hadn't bothered him before

Mrs. Schraalenburgh handed out the papers. Julio knew what was causing his pains, but he didn't know what could be bothering his grandmother. Maybe she worried too much about the fate of the characters in the soap operas she watched every day.

"All right, everyone. Put down your pencils and we'll discuss the questions," called out Mrs. Schraalenburgh. "These word problems are one type of math that will be covered on the statewide test. You didn't find them too hard now, did you?" she asked.

Hard? Julio hadn't answered a single one. There were still eight more problems that he hadn't even read.

Cricket raised her hand. "You mean they actually give us the answer to every question and all we have to do is pick it out from the wrong ones?" she asked.

"That's right. Or occasionally they try to fool you and not give you the answer at all. Then you should mark 'none of the above' or 'don't have enough information.'"

"So it's really like a game," said Cricket with a

huge smile on her face. "It's like being on a quiz show on TV."

"That's a great attitude," Mrs. Schraalenburgh said, beaming back at her student.

"The only problem is, no one is going to win any prizes here," complained Lucas.

"Education is its own reward," Mrs. Schraalenburgh told him.

The students began going over the problems one by one. The trout was bigger than the lobster, there were eighty ounces in the five-pound bag of sugar, and so on and so forth.

Zoe Mitchell, who was every bit as smart as Cricket, raised her hand. "Are all the math questions this easy?" she asked. "Or did you just give us some simple ones for a start?"

"If you read each question carefully, you'll find that you'll be able to answer most of them. And that's the whole key to test taking. Read slowly and carefully. Be sure you understand what the question is asking you. When you don't know the answer, skip that question and move on to the next one.

You can come back and reread the difficult question afterward instead of spending too much time worrying about what you don't know."

Julio looked down at his paper. He had marked each question with the correct answer as they'd gone over them. But he worried. Julio had been so busy thinking about the topics covered in the sentences that he hadn't even answered a single one.

Reluctantly he raised his hand. "How much time do we get to do the test?" he asked.

"Don't worry about the time. You'll have more than enough," Mrs. Schraalenburgh said.

Enough time for Cricket. Enough time for Lucas. Enough time for Zoe, Julio thought. And just enough time for me to fail this test. And then what? Next year when all his classmates were in fifth grade, he'd probably be back repeating fourth grade. And they certainly wouldn't put him in Mrs. Schraalenburgh's class again. Just because he could pronounce her name, and could spell it now too, didn't mean that he was bright. In fact, today he felt very stupid.

6 · Ramon's Test

"**A**s soon as my brother gets his license, he's going to buy a car. And then we can take trips to all sorts of places," Julio promised Lucas.

Lucas's family owned a car, but still Lucas was impressed. It was one thing for a parent to go driving and another for a brother. Especially a brother as friendly as Ramon. Julio and Lucas knew they could both look forward to good times when Ramon took them riding.

"I have a list of places where we can go," said Julio. He began to rattle off sites that would no longer be so distant once he had someone to drive him: "That big amusement park in Woodbury, the aquarium, going to the beach in the summer. It's going to be fantastic."

"Well, your brother has a job so he can't take you driving just any old time. And sometimes he'll want to go off with his friends without us tagging along," said Lucas.

"Aw. He'll squeeze us in even if he has friends in the car," said Julio confidently.

"Not if the friend is a girl," said Lucas, who had learned about such things from TV and the movies.

"No way, José," said Julio. "Ramon takes his driving test in a couple of days, and he's already been looking at cars. I bet we can go driving with him by next week."

"That's okay by me," said Lucas. "I hope you're right."

Ramon was scheduled to take his driving test on the first Tuesday of February. On the morning of the test, Julio was surprised to see his brother looking rattled. He'd buttoned his shirt wrong when he was getting dressed and he didn't even notice. It was their grandmother who called the mistake to his attention when he came into the kitchen to fix himself some breakfast.

Almost at once, Ramon spilled the orange juice when he was pouring himself a glass. And then he burned the bagel he was fixing in the little toaster oven. The whole kitchen smelled of overtoasted bagel. Mrs. Sanchez opened the window to clear the air.

"Hey, it's twenty degrees outside," Nelson complained. "We're all going to freeze to death."

"Put on a sweatshirt," his mother advised him.

"At least it didn't snow," Ramon said.

Julio remembered that in addition to thinking about the driving test, Ramon had been checking the weather report every day. Snow would just make everything that much harder. There might be ice on the road, which could make a car skid. Or if it had snowed the day before, there would be piles of snow along the curbs that would make parking much more difficult, if not impossible.

Mrs. Sanchez closed the window. "Take another bagel," she told Ramon. "You'll drive better if you aren't hungry as well as nervous."

"Hey, man. You'll ace the test. Stop worrying," Nelson said.

"Tomorrow is another day," commented their grandmother in Spanish.

Julio knew she meant that if Ramon didn't get his license today, he'd have another chance. But Julio also knew that was the last thing Ramon liked hearing. He didn't want another chance. He'd been waiting for this license since before Julio was even born. Ramon wanted it now.

"I know you can do it. You'll pass. You'll see," he said to Ramon as he gave his brother a hug.

"Thanks, kid. I'll take you for the first ride after I pass the test and after I buy a car."

"I knew it," said Julio, beaming. "Can Lucas come along too?"

"What about me?" asked their grandmother.

"Tomorrow is another day," Ramon told her in Spanish, and everyone, except their grandmother, laughed.

Mrs. Sanchez left for work. The boys left for school. And their grandmother was left with the breakfast dishes and her favorite TV programs to help her pass the hours. Even though she spoke so little English, she seemed to understand enough to follow what was being said on the screen.

One didn't need to know any spoken language to figure out the result of Ramon's test. He walked into the apartment at the end of the day and his whole body gave the news. Bad news. He had failed the road test. He was unhappy and he was angry, too.

"How could that happen?" Nelson asked. "You know how to drive."

"The examiner said I went too fast. I zipped into the parking space in one try. I made the U-turn without any problem. But he said I didn't stop long enough at the stop sign. And he said I pulled out too quickly from the parking space. But I know I was good. I should have passed."

Ramon pounded his fist on the kitchen table. "I'm a very good driver even without all the practice that the other kids got. I should have passed the test; I know I should have."

"What about the others?" asked Mrs. Sanchez. "How did they do?"

"That's the crazy thing," said Ramon. "Lucy and Caroline both passed. Lucy is a nervous wreck when she drives. She has to chew gum or she can't even get the car started. She says the gum relaxes her. And one day when she forgot to bring any gum to school, she wouldn't even take her turn at the wheel. She's nuts, but she passed."

"What about the other boy who's in your group?" asked Julio.

"Jeff? He failed too. It really doesn't make sense. He isn't as good as me, but he drives better than either of the girls. And I drove the best. So why did I fail?"

"I'll tell you something," Mrs. Sanchez said. "I

didn't want to mention it before because maybe it wasn't true. But I was discussing the driving test with Simon, who works at the front desk at the motel. He told me that more often than not, the examiners automatically fail boys who are taking the test for the first time. It isn't a matter of how well you drive, but statistically more males get into accidents than females. And they figure that the failure will make you be more careful in the future and perhaps prevent careless driving."

"That's terrible!" said Ramon. "Besides that, it's sexist. It's illegal. It's dishonest." But Julio noticed that his brother's mood seemed to change slightly. It was as if what his mother said took away some of the pain of failure. He was still annoyed, but not at himself. If all boys taking the test had a greater chance of failure than girls, it meant he wasn't a bad driver after all. It was just the way the Motor Vehicle Bureau did things.

"And let me tell you something else," Mrs. Sanchez said. "Simon told me that his wife failed her driving test six times before she finally passed."

Nelson let out a whistle.

"She had to be a rotten driver to fail that many times," said Ramon.

"No, Simon says she just panicked every time she sat beside the examiner. And now that she's had her license, she drives without any trouble at all. She's never had an accident."

"How long has she been driving. Two weeks?" asked Nelson.

"No," said Mrs. Sanchez. "Twenty-seven years. She even drove across the country once when she and Simon were going to a family wedding in Colorado and he had broken his arm and couldn't drive at all."

"Talk, talk, talk. When do you do your work at the motel, if you talk so much to that Simon?" Julio's grandmother wanted to know.

"I get a fifteen-minute coffee break twice a day," said Mrs. Sanchez to her mother. "Talking with Simon has fewer calories than a cup of coffee and a muffin."

The mention of food reminded Julio that he was hungry. "What's for supper?" he asked.

While they were eating supper, Mrs. Sanchez remembered one more thing that Simon had told her. "No matter how many times you take the driving test, once you have a license, that's it. No one knows if you took the test once or a dozen times. There isn't a number painted on the back of your car to inform people about your past driving history."

Ramon let out a laugh. "The only cars that have numbers are race cars," he said. He took a second helping of chicken. There was no question that he was feeling loads better than he had when he returned home earlier.

"You know what Mr. Hughes said this morning before we took the road test? He said even with lessons and a license, you don't really learn how to drive until you have the license and are using a car on a regular basis in all sorts of traffic situations. It's really weird. You can't drive until you get a license, but you don't learn to drive until you get one."

"You can't drive until you get a car," Nelson reminded his brother.

"That's not going to be a problem," Ramon said

confidently. "But keep your fingers crossed that it doesn't snow on February fourteenth," he told his family.

"February fourteenth is Valentine's Day," said Julio. "What's happening then?"

"That's the date that I scheduled for my next road test," said Ramon. "I sure hope I don't need to take seven of them like Simon's wife."

Julio chewed thoughtfully on his chicken. He always looked up to Ramon, but tonight he studied his brother with more than his usual admiration. Even though Ramon had failed his road test, he already was cheerful and positive about retaking the test. He could even joke about it. Usually Julio tried to imitate Ramon's attitude toward life. But in this matter of testing, it wasn't going to work. If he had to repeat the fourth-grade standardized tests seven times, he wouldn't be promoted to the next grade for seven years. He'd even end up in the *Guinness Book of World Records* as the oldest fourth grader in history. He'd just have to do well the first time, he decided. But of course it was easier said than done.

7 · Practice Tests

While searching the library for a nonfiction book for his next report, Eddie Kovacs, a student in one of the other fourth-grade classes, had found a book about superstitions. Amazingly, there had been a section about school situations, and it gave suggestions to help you pass an exam. Of course, he checked the book out. He sat with the book open in front of him in the school lunchroom, which was a first for Eddie. And before long, every fourth grader in every class had heard about what they could do to improve their testing ability. Some of the suggestions were impossible.

Don't shave.

"Perfect," said Lucas. "None of us shave, so we'll all do fine on the state tests."

"I don't think it counts," said Cricket. "Don't shave means don't do something you would ordinarily have done."

"How do you know that?" Lucas asked her. "It's just a matter of interpretation. I think I'm right."

"Well you're not," said Cricket with her usual certainty. "What else does the book tell you to do?"

"Wear your socks and your underwear inside out," Lucas reported.

"How are you going to turn everything inside out when you get to school?" Cricket wanted to know. "The line at the girls' room would be awfully long if all the fourth-grade girls were waiting to go inside and turn their underwear inside out."

"Do it at home before you come to school," suggested Julio. This was one thing he could do, but he wondered how it could possibly help him.

"Well, I think that's just plain stupid," said Cricket. "I'm not going to wear my clothes inside out. Besides, I know I'll do great on the test without any of these silly tricks."

"Anything else?" asked Zoe.

"The book said to use the same pencil you used the last time you passed a test or else use a new one that never made a mistake."

Everyone in Mrs. Schraalenburgh's class agreed that they could and would do that.

Even Cricket.

Lately Mrs. Schraalenburgh had given her students new quiet time activities. Sometimes she handed out crossword puzzles. Other times she permitted the students to break into small groups and play games like Scrabble or Hangman together. It was no surprise to Julio that Cricket was familiar with these activities. "I always play Scrabble with my grandmother when she comes to visit," she told her classmates.

"That's wonderful," said Mrs. Schraalenburgh.

It didn't bother Julio that he couldn't play anything except card games like rummy and war with his grandmother. But then one afternoon Mrs. Schraalenburgh said, "Do you know why we're playing all these word games lately?"

No one did, not even Cricket.

"It's because games like these are another way to practice and improve your spelling. The spelling bees that we've had this year have also been a method to test your spelling skill."

"Well, we still need written practice questions in spelling to prepare for the test," Cricket insisted.

"Don't worry," Mrs. Schraalenburgh said. "You're going to do that tomorrow."

And sure enough, the next day Mrs. Schraalenburgh gave out sheets with spelling questions. Each question consisted of a list of four words. One might or might not be misspelled. The students were to examine the words and make a decision. Was one word wrong or not?

Julio studied the sheet in front of him:

1. a) beyond
   b) purchace
   c) simply
   d) picnic
   e) no mistakes

2. a) knee
   b) stomache
   c) shoulder
   d) finger
   e) no mistakes

3. a) mountain
   b) ocean
   c) field
   d) islend
   e) no mistakes

4. a) weather
   b) tornado

c) huricane

d) flood

e) no mistakes

"This is fun," Cricket called out. "It's easier than any spelling test I've ever taken."

"I'm glad you're enjoying it," said Mrs. Schraalenburgh. "But remember, you must never ever call out, especially if this was the actual test that you were taking."

"Fun?" Julio mumbled to himself. Poor Cricket must lead a very boring life if this was her idea of fun. As far as he was concerned, all the words looked fine to him. How was he supposed to guess which might be misspelled? And it seemed pretty stupid to make mistakes on purpose just to trick the fourth graders.

Later in the day, Mrs. Schraalenburgh gave out a different set of sheets. "This will test your study skills," she told the students. "I think you'll find these very simple after all the lessons we've had here in class and in the school library."

Julio looked down at his sheet.

Choose the name or word that would appear first, if they were arranged alphabetically:

1. a) Jones, Ruth
    b) Jones, Rose
    c) Jones, Joan
    d) Jones, Ralph

2. a) pancake
    b) powder
    c) pan
    d) paint

In which book would you look to discover where France is located?

a) cookbook
b) calendar
c) atlas
d) telephone book

Finally there was a question that Julio thought was easy. Imagine looking for France in a cookbook! The only thing you'd find there would be French fries.

8 · Say "Cheese"

While preparation for the standardized tests was something new for the fourth graders, many of their other activities were exactly like those of years past. There was the annual police department assembly program about bicycle safety. The format changed slightly from year to year, but the message about always wearing helmets and wearing reflectors if you're out after dark remained the same. There was also the annual visit to the local high school to watch the older students during their final dress rehearsal of the annual musical they produced. Every year Julio hoped he'd run into his brothers at the high school.

"Don't you see them enough at home?" Lucas asked Julio.

"Sure," admitted Julio. "But I've never seen them at the high school."

"Big deal. They'll look just the way they do at your house. Besides, if they don't try out for the musical, they can't be in it," Lucas pointed out.

But Julio always hoped he'd get a glimpse of either Ramon or Nelson as the elementary-school kids walked down the hallway toward the auditorium.

This year the high school musical was *The Pajama Game*. The audience was made up of young elementary-school students and elderly residents of the local senior center. Julio overheard a couple of fourth-grade teachers complaining to each other after the show.

"This was a colossal waste of time," said one.

"Especially at this time of year," said the other.

Julio realized that he probably hadn't learned anything new during the two hours he'd sat in the high school auditorium. But come to think of it, the word *colossal* might show up on the vocabulary part of the standardized test. And besides, attending the show had been a lot of fun. He'd walked up the aisle humming one of the melodies to himself. *Seven and a half cents, seven and a half cents . . .*

On the bus returning to their elementary school, Mrs. Schraalenburgh told the students a bit about labor unions and workers uniting to get higher wages. So, come to think of it, Julio suddenly realized, he had learned something new that day after all.

One thing that happened every year was that school photographs were taken. Mrs. Schraalenburgh reminded her students on Friday. "Everyone, please dress appropriately for your pictures on Monday. Our principal, Mr. Herbertson, suggests that boys will look their most handsome in a white shirt and tie. Girls, see that your hair is combed away from your face so we can really see you."

Cricket raised her hand. "What should girls wear?"

"Oh, Cricket," said Mrs. Schraalenburgh with a sigh.

It was a silly question, Julio thought. Cricket just loved to hear her own voice.

"This isn't the first time you've had your school photo taken," Mrs. Schraalenburgh pointed out. "What did you wear last year?"

"I wore my green velveteen dress. But it doesn't fit me anymore."

"Whatever you wear will be fine," said Mrs. Schraalenburgh. "Remember, in addition to your individual photograph, there will be a class portrait with everyone in it. It's a lovely souvenir of the grade, and you'll want to look your best." She smiled at her students. "I have an album with the class portrait from every year of my teaching career."

"How many pictures do you have?" Lucas called out.

Julio knew that was his way of asking how many years Mrs. Schraalenburgh had been teaching. It was also a way to figure out their teacher's age. Fifteen pictures would mean fifteen years. You could add that to the age their teacher probably graduated from college and you'd have an answer. It was sort of like one of the practice math questions.

Mrs. Schraalenburgh guessed what Lucas had in mind too. She answered him by saying, "Why, Lucas, I have class pictures going all the way back to the time of the American Revolution."

Even someone who wasn't good in social studies knew that Mrs. Schraalenburgh was making a joke!

On Monday morning Julio arrived at school wearing his white shirt, a necktie, and a jacket that had formerly belonged to Nelson. He'd admired himself in the bathroom mirror at home and knew he looked sharp. His hair was slicked back with some of Ramon's special mousse, too. When he came into the classroom, he saw that most of his classmates looked pretty neat as well. They should have dressed up when they went to the high school, he thought now. Most of the men among the senior citizens had come wearing jackets and ties.

"Oh, Lucas. You didn't wear a white shirt," Cricket called out as Lucas removed his winter jacket. Sure enough, Lucas was wearing a black long-sleeved T-shirt with a fierce head of a dinosaur on it.

Lucas shrugged. "I forgot," he admitted.

Lucas wasn't the only one. Peter Saunders, Alex Collins, Steve Greenfield, and Bobby Evans were also wearing T-shirts with and without pictures.

Mrs. Schraalenburgh shook her head when she saw them. "This always happens when the school photo session takes place on Monday. If it was tomorrow, I could have reminded you just before you left for home. Oh, well, so be it," she said.

Julio had an idea. "I could take off my shirt and tie and jacket and lend it to the other boys," he offered.

"Then what will you wear when you get your picture taken?" Cricket wanted to know. "Your underwear?"

Everyone giggled at that comment.

"No, silly," said Julio. "We'll take turns. The photographer only does one picture at a time. After I pose for my picture, I could take my shirt off and Lucas could put it on. And after Lucas, Peter, and then Steve, Bobby, and Alex. We're all about the same size, more or less."

"That's a smart idea," said Zoe, smiling at Julio.

"It would be a good plan," admitted Mrs. Schraalenburgh, "but I think the photographer takes all the girls' pictures and then all the boys'. There just won't be enough time for each boy to change into and out of your shirt. You'd have to be like Clark Kent dressing rapidly to become Superman. And you know the photographer keeps to a very tight schedule. He has to photograph every child in the school today."

"Why does he have to do all the girls and then all the boys?" Julio asked. "If he took a boy's picture and then a girl's, there'd be time for the next boy to put on my shirt. And then if the next person photographed was another girl, there'd be time for another boy to put on my shirt."

"Julio, I give you A plus for common sense," said Mrs. Schraalenburgh, beaming at her student. And so that was exactly what was done for Class 4S. The photographer was told that for this class, he would have to alternate girls and boys as he took his pictures. Julio stood in the assigned spot with the bright light shining on his face and gave a grin, even before the photographer could remind him to say cheese. As soon as the camera flashed, Julio moved aside for one of the girls. He quickly removed his jacket and shirt and slipped his necktie over his head without actually untying it. Ramon had helped him at home and he didn't think he could redo it by himself. He handed his clothing over to Peter. Eventually everyone in the class had been photographed.

"Wait till my mom hears that my clothes got into so many pictures," Julio said, grinning.

As for the class portrait, Mrs. Schraalenburgh arranged the boys in T-shirts to stand in the back row, half hidden by their classmates who were more appropriately dressed. Julio had a spot right in front, standing tall and proud in his white shirt, necktie, and Nelson's old jacket.

"Say cheese," the photographer said once again.

Julio thought it must be very boring to repeat the same thing over and over and over again all day long. And tomorrow the photographer would probably be at another school telling other students the same thing: "Say cheese."

"Gorgonzola," called out Lucas.

Luckily the photographer quickly snapped the shutter before everyone turned to ask Lucas the same question. "What's that?"

Even Cricket didn't know what Gorgonzola was. "Is that the type of dinosaur on your shirt?" she asked him.

"It's a kind of cheese," said Lucas. "The photographer didn't tell us what kind of cheese he wanted us to say."

"Gorgonzola? It sounds gross," said Alex.

"You could have said Swiss," suggested Connie Alf.

"Or American. I like that the best."

"I like cheddar," another voice called out.

"Enough cheeses," said Mrs. Schraalenburgh as the class walked back to their room. "You're making me hungry, and we still have an hour to go until lunchtime."

"I wonder what's for lunch in the cafeteria today?" asked Bobby.

"I know," Julio told him. He always knew what they were serving because he looked forward to the school lunch each day. "It's macaroni and cheese," he announced.

Julio sighed. He was getting hungry. He wondered what Gorgonzola tasted like. He'd be willing to try it, but he hoped it wouldn't ever turn up as one of their spelling words. Who in fourth grade would know something like that? Even Cricket would get it wrong.

9 · Happy Birthday, Julio

Even though the standardized tests were uppermost in Julio's mind much of the time, especially when he was at school, he didn't think of them every minute of the day. Sometimes on the weekend when he was busy playing soccer with a bunch of kids, going to a movie with his brothers, or playing over at Lucas's house, he forgot about them altogether. After all, there was more to life than school and tests. For example, there was his birthday at the end of February to look forward to.

Last year on his birthday, Julio had gotten a brand-new bicycle. Until then he'd been using a beat-up old bike that had belonged first to Ramon and then to Nelson. It was secondhand when Ramon got it, so no one knew how old the bike really was. It was certainly a lot older than Julio. The tires had been patched countless times and the chain fell off frequently, most of the paint had worn off, and there were rusty places too. Still, it got him from his house to Lucas's, and he could ride it to the library or the pizza shop. But on the morning of his ninth birthday, Ramon, Nelson, and his mother made him close his eyes and then walk down the stairs of their apartment building to the storage area on the ground floor before opening them again. There before him was a brand-new, bright red bike. He'd been stunned.

"Is that for me?" Julio had asked in amazement. Birthday presents in his family were usually items of clothing and maybe some small plaything. Nothing so big and expensive as a new bike had ever been among anyone's gifts.

"This is your birthday present for this year and next year and the year after," said Nelson. And Julio knew he wasn't joking. Such an expensive present couldn't be expected ever again.

"I'll take very good care of it and it will last for the rest of my life," he told his mother and brothers. "I can't wait to ride it over to Lucas's house. He'll be so surprised. He always teases me about my old bike."

"Here's one more gift," said Mrs. Sanchez. She handed Julio a gift-wrapped box and when he opened it, he pulled out a new helmet.

That had been last year. He knew he couldn't possibly expect to top the thrill of the new bike. Still, a birthday was a special day. His mother always prepared his favorite dish for the family. He hoped she'd buy a cake even if his grandmother couldn't eat it. He loved blowing out the candles and making a wish. Yes, the thought of his approaching birthday was a wonderful diversion for Julio, though lately his stomach had become nervous, like that of his grandmother, and from time to time gave him an unexpected jolt.

On February fourteenth Ramon took his second road test. Julio had told him about the book of superstitions and suggested to his brother that he not shave on the morning of the test.

"My test is on a Wednesday and I never shave on Wednesday," said Ramon. He shaved three times a week these days: Tuesday, Friday, and Sunday.

"Good," said Julio. "You could wear your underwear inside out too," he suggested.

"Maybe that works in fourth grade, but not for me," Ramon said. "I'm going to pass because I know how to drive."

And so he went off and took his driving test and did pass. He came home smiling proudly.

"I did it!" he said. "And tomorrow after work, I'm going to put the deposit down on a car that I saw over at Tony's Used Car Lot."

"Saw?" said Nelson, who had gone with Ramon on one of his car-hunting expeditions. "You were hugging and kissing that car like she was a pretty girl."

"Maybe you should give her a name," said their grandmother.

"It's a fifteen-year-old Ford with an awful lot of miles on it," said Ramon. "It doesn't need a name."

"Flora the Ford," said Nelson, ignoring Ramon. "The love of your life."

"Shouldn't we celebrate?" asked Julio. "Let's have a party."

"What do you want to celebrate?" asked Mrs. Sanchez.

"Ramon's passing his driving test. It's a big deal. He's the first person in our family to do it. And he's going to be the first to own a car. That's a very big deal."

"One party at a time is enough," Mrs. Sanchez said, which sounded a bit strange to Julio. But he decided that the donuts that Ramon had brought home, despite the fact that he'd been told not to, must equal a party in his mother's mind.

Julio's tenth birthday fell ten days later, on a Saturday. When he was eating breakfast, he was given three wrapped packages. One held socks. In another package was a T-shirt. And the third package held a pair of woolen mittens that his grandmother had knit for him. His family hadn't been joking when they said the bike was his gift for the next three years. Julio had known not to expect anything big. But three packages of clothing were pretty slim pickings as far as birthday presents went.

"I arranged my schedule to work only this morning, and when I get back I'm taking you for a ride in Flora," Ramon announced. Despite himself, he had begun calling the car by the silly name that Nelson had suggested.

Julio brightened. "Can I call Lucas and have him come, too?" he asked. Going off in the car with his brother and Lucas would certainly make the day seem more festive, more like a birthday celebration.

"Oh, no," sputtered Ramon. "I—I—I may have to make a few stops and pick up some stuff and there won't be room in the car for other passengers."

"What kind of stuff?" asked Julio eagerly. Maybe there was some other bigger and better birthday present for him after all.

"Well, I'm getting a new tire for the car, for one thing," said Ramon. "I noticed that the right front tire seems very worn, and it's dangerous to drive with it."

Well, a tire certainly didn't qualify as a birthday present.

Saturday morning was cleaning time at Julio's home, and so even though it was his birthday, he helped his mother with various chores: removing the sheets from everyone's bed and taking the laundry down to the machines in the basement. Julio didn't complain aloud, but he wasn't overjoyed. What kind of a birthday was this? he wondered. Socks and mittens and laundry?

He watched Nelson hurry through his chores. He didn't have to work today and he had a date with a girl in his class. "I forgot it was your birthday when Coralee and I made this date," he said. "You probably wouldn't like the movie we're going to anyway," he added.

Julio had never seen a movie he didn't like. But he knew that Nelson had a thing for Coralee and this was the first time he was taking her out.

At noon Ramon returned home.

"Are you ready?" he asked Julio.

"Yep," said Julio. "Could we get lunch out? Pizza or hot dogs or something?" he asked.

"Here," Ramon said, throwing an apple to Julio. "If you're hungry, eat this. I just had a bite at work."

Apples were all well and good most times, but on your birthday? Julio felt really down. But riding in Flora was still a novelty, and so he cheered up when he sat in the front seat next to Ramon. He was glad his brother didn't insist that he sit in the back the way Lucas's mother always did. He watched carefully when Ramon put the key in the ignition and started the car. It occurred to him that if he looked at Ramon when they drove, he could learn from him all about driving. That way when the time came for him to take the road test for getting a license, it wouldn't be so hard.

"First stop, Sears," said Ramon. "I'm lucky they're having a big tire sale."

Julio was glad none of his classmates knew today

was his birthday. Otherwise, when he got to school on Monday, someone was sure to ask him what he got. Socks, a T-shirt, mittens, and a new tire for his brother's car. Ugh.

After leaving Sears, Ramon drove a bit and then parked the car. "See how good I am at parallel parking?" he bragged to Julio. Then he suggested that Julio wait in the car instead of accompanying him on his next errand. "Someone might see my new tire and want to steal it," he said.

Julio sat in the car wondering why Ramon hadn't put it in the trunk. Then Lucas could have come along. He tried turning on the car radio but discovered that unless the car was running, the radio didn't work. He watched the people walking along the street and sighed. What next? he wondered. He was feeling hungry. The apple had not really filled him up. This was not a particularly special day after all.

Ramon came walking toward the car carrying a shopping bag.

"What's inside?" asked Julio.

"Oh it's just something Mom asked me to pick up

for her," Ramon said. He started the car and headed for home.

"That was an awfully short ride," complained Julio when they reached their house.

"I know, but Mom is waiting for this," said Ramon, taking out the shopping bag from the backseat.

"What is it?" Julio asked.

"Oh, just something she needs," Ramon answered.

"Well, can we go off somewhere after you give it to her?" Julio asked.

"I don't know," said Ramon. "I might be busy."

"But you promised me a ride," complained Julio. He thought he'd always remember his tenth birthday as the most disappointing and boring day of his life.

He was wrong. When he got upstairs, he discovered their apartment was filled with all the boys in his class. "Surprise!" they shouted.

Julio's jaw dropped open. He'd never had any kind of a birthday party before, at least not a party with guests who weren't related to him. And suddenly here were eleven boys from school, who had come to celebrate with him, sitting on the sofa and the floor.

"How did you know it was my birthday and where I lived?" he asked them.

"We've been planning this for ages," said Mrs. Sanchez, laughing with delight. "We really surprised you, didn't we? I was afraid that I gave it away the night you wanted to make a party for Ramon."

"I helped," said Lucas proudly.

"That's right," said Ramon. "Lucas was able to get everyone's phone number so we could call and invite them. And he promised he'd watch that no one gave away the secret at school."

"No one did," said Julio.

"I threatened them," Lucas bragged. "I said anyone who gave away the surprise couldn't come."

"It worked," said Peter Saunders. He was one of the boys who had worn Julio's shirt, tie, and jacket for his class picture.

"Who's hungry?" asked Ramon.

"I am!" twelve boys called out at once.

Julio laughed. "Now I know why you wouldn't buy me any lunch," he said to Ramon.

Mrs. Sanchez came out of the kitchen holding a

huge pot. "There's plenty for everyone. I hope you have big appetites because I made two pots full of this. It's Julio's favorite."

"And mine, too," called out a voice in Spanish. It was Julio's grandmother.

Even before his mother removed the lid from the pot, Julio knew what was inside: rice and beans and chicken in a spicy tomato sauce. Usually he loved this dish, but today he worried what the boys would think. None of them ever touched the baked beans that were served with hot dogs at school.

"Eat the beans and you're a gas machine," Lucas had announced to Julio and their other classmates back in second grade. Then he'd made a funny sound with his mouth, imitating a fart. The boys were two years older, but still no one, except Julio, dared to eat the school beans.

Julio and his classmates squeezed around the table. It was a tight fit, but none of the guests complained. There wasn't room for the bread, so Ramon walked about handing out slices to everyone. Mrs. Sanchez filled their bowls from the steaming casserole.

Grandma sat on the sofa with her helping. They all dug into the food and no one complained about the danger of eating beans. In fact, all of the boys asked for and received seconds. The food was very good!

Except for Lucas, none of the boys had ever visited Julio's home before. Most of his classmates lived in big houses and had their own bedrooms. Julio was nervous that the boys would think his family's apartment was too tiny and his grandmother's Spanish was weird. But after everyone ate their lunch, they listened as she taught them how to sing "Happy Birthday" in Spanish. They all sang along before Julio cut into the ice-cream cake, shaped like a car. It was what Ramon had picked up in the shopping bag when he had taken Julio out for a ride. Julio looked around. There were eleven boys from school, he made twelve, Ramon and his mother made fourteen. "Can Abuela have a piece?" he asked.

"No diets on birthdays," his grandmother told him firmly.

"Even if it isn't your birthday?" asked Julio.

"Of course," she told him.

Fifteen portions and one to go into the freezer for Nelson. Carefully Julio cut sixteen pieces of cake. He did a good job of it and the cake was delicious.

The fourth-grade boys all admired Julio's bedroom because even though he shared the space with his two brothers, the walls were decorated with neat posters of everyone's favorite sports figures.

There was a huge pile of gifts for Julio to open. They included two new books, a book of puzzles and a jigsaw puzzle with five hundred pieces (which Julio thought might take him a hundred years to complete), a harmonica, a flashlight, a new backpack, a pocket calculator, a mini transistor radio, and a kite that needed to be assembled before it could be flown. No more clothes, Julio thought delightedly as he opened each package. The last box contained a bank in the shape of a car.

"You can use that to start saving for a real car," suggested Ramon. Everyone laughed at that. It would be a long time before Julio could buy a car of his own.

When the final package was opened and admired, Julio wondered what they would do next. The apartment was too small for playing any kind of games.

"Now comes the best part of this party," said Ramon.

"What's that?" asked Julio, wondering what other surprise was in store for him.

"I'm going to teach you all how to change a tire."

"Wow."

"Neat."

"Fantastic."

"Super."

"No kidding!"

And Ramon, accompanied by twelve fourth-grade boys, went downstairs to put the new tire on his car.

Julio knew he'd never forget his tenth birthday!

10 · The Big Day

R eady or not, the time had arrived for the fourth-grade tests. The language arts test was today and the math part would be the day after tomorrow.

"You are all ready. Every one of you," said Mrs. Schraalenburgh to her students.

Julio knew that football coaches and baseball managers gave pep talks to their players before the start of a game. He had the feeling that Mrs. Schraalenburgh was doing the same thing.

When he had gotten dressed this morning, he had made a point of turning his underwear inside out. What could it hurt? he wondered. And besides, no one could see. But when he got to school and listened to his classmates chattering, he discovered that just about everyone had done the same thing.

"Not me," said Cricket. "I don't need to do stupid things like that to pass a test."

"Oh, come on, Cricket. Confess. No one can see your darn underwear, so we can only guess. But I bet you did put it on inside out just like everyone else," said Lucas.

Cricket blushed. "Only my socks," she said, looking down at her feet.

Julio decided he needed all the help he could get, even if it was something as silly as wearing his underwear inside out. The only problem was that his stomach was bothering him. It had bothered him the evening before, too. Julio guessed it was nerves that caused the pains he was feeling. Shortly after he arrived in school, he went to the boys' room, hoping it would help him feel better. He hadn't realized how difficult it would be with his briefs turned the wrong way.

Now he was back in his seat. The students were sitting and waiting till the hands on the clock in the front of the room showed 10 A.M. There was still half an hour to go, but Mrs. Schraalenburgh knew better than to try and distract them with an extra math lesson or even reading aloud. So she said that they could speak together, but to keep their voices low. Lucas leaned across the aisle and grinned at Julio. "Did you sharpen all your pencils?" he asked.

Julio looked down at the pencils on his desk. A spasm of pain passed through his belly. The awful feeling in his stomach just didn't want to go away. He'd felt it several times in recent weeks, but today was the worst ever.

"It's just nerves," Mrs. Sanchez said when Julio told her he couldn't eat any breakfast.

"Relax," Ramon said, patting Julio on the back. "I passed my test and you're going to pass yours. The only difference is that I got a car as a result. All you'll get is relief when today is over."

"It won't even be over after today. There's the second part of the test too," Julio said.

"Come on now. You must eat something," Mrs. Sanchez had insisted.

But for once, Julio, who was always hungry, had no appetite.

"Could I stay home with Abuela today?" he pleaded with his mother.

"Julio. That's silly. If you stay home, you'll miss this test that you've been telling me about. And you'll only have to make it up on another day. Better just get it over with."

Julio knew his mother was right. He only wished his stomach wasn't giving him such a hard time. Now, sitting in his classroom seat, he took a deep breath and told himself to keep calm.

Suddenly the door to their room opened. In walked Mr. Herbertson. Julio had a wild thought. Perhaps the principal had come to announce that the exam had been canceled. That would be about the best news in the world, he knew. He sat at attention, waiting hopefully. Though he had never had a run-in with the principal, he prayed he never would. Mr. Herbertson had dark, piercing eyes that made you think he could see right inside your brain. It was silly, of course. No one could do that. But if ever anyone could, it would be Mr. Herbertson with his X-ray-like eyes.

The principal walked to the front of the room. He didn't need to call for the class's attention. He had it. Everyone was sitting in the same alert posture as Julio. When Mr. Herbertson spoke, everyone listened. Even Mrs. Schraalenburgh was standing straighter.

Mr. Herbertson looked around the room. Then he began speaking. "In a few minutes you will be taking a very important examination. I want each of you to do your very best so that we can be proud of you. And while you are taking this test, there is to be no speaking, no whispering, no squirming about in your seats. No bad behavior of any sort."

"No breathing," Lucas whispered to the students sitting around him.

Mr. Herbertson didn't hear Lucas's comment, but

he did hear the nervous giggles of those students who had.

"Am I making myself perfectly clear?" the principal demanded to know. "There is to be no fooling around, no talking, no whispering, no anything at all."

Those words must have been more than Lucas could accept because in a much louder and clearer voice he called out, "Give me liberty or give me death."

"Who said that?" demanded Mr. Herbertson.

Everyone in the room, including Mrs. Schraalenburgh, knew the answer to that question.

"Patrick Henry," Lucas called out.

Mr. Herbertson's face turned red with annoyance. "I hope this isn't an indication of your behavior this morning," he said over the laughter of the fourth graders.

Any other day Mrs. Schraalenburgh would have scolded Lucas. But now instead she let him get away by saying, "I'm afraid we're all a bit tense this morning." She looked in Lucas's direction as she added, "Don't worry about these students. They'll all behave and they'll do just fine, too."

Mrs. Schraalenburgh usually had a way of calming Julio. But this morning, he really couldn't relax. He felt another sharp pain in his gut. Mrs. Schraalenburgh referred to the little boxes that the students were to fill in with their pencils to show which answer they had selected as *bubbles*. Julio felt as if there was a pencil with a very sharp point inside his stomach filling in a bubble. Nerves, he told himself once again as he watched Mr. Herbertson walk out of the room. The principal was probably off to make his little speech about good behavior in the other fourth-grade classrooms.

"I wish it was ten o'clock already," said Cricket.

Julio looked over at her desk. There were four new pencils with perfectly sharpened points ready for her to fill in the correct bubbles on her exam sheet. Julio fidgeted in his seat, trying to find a position that lessened his stomach pain. He felt like he had to go to the bathroom again, but he knew he couldn't ask to leave the room again so soon, especially with the exam just about to begin. He wished the test was over and that he was home in bed, curled up under his blanket. He gritted his teeth so as not to call out when the pain in his stomach came again. He envied his classmates. They could just sit waiting, talking and laughing. It seemed he was the only one with such a serious case of nerves.

When the hands on the clock reached ten to ten, Mrs. Schraalenburgh opened one of the drawers in her desk and took out a large manila envelope. Every eye in the class watched as she extracted the test booklets from the envelope. Carefully she counted out the correct number and put piles of tests on the front desks.

"Take one and pass these back," she instructed. "Place them on the center of your desk. No one is to open his or her booklet until I tell you," she warned.

Quietly the booklets were passed around. Soon every desk had the same white pages stapled together.

"You all know the procedure," Mrs. Schraalenburgh said. "We've gone over it enough times. When I give the signal, you will open your booklets and turn to the first page. Read each question carefully and mark your answer neatly. If you're not certain of an answer, skip it and return to it later. Don't spend too much time on any one question or you won't be able to finish the exam. Remember to fill in the bubbles neatly."

Everything Mrs. Schraalenburgh said had been told to the class many times before. Nevertheless, it was reassuring to hear it all again.

Mrs. Schraalenburgh turned to look at the clock. The big hand was just about to touch the twelve. It was ten o'clock.

"Open your booklets," said Mrs. Schraalenburgh. "You may begin."

Julio and his classmates opened to the first page. Julio picked up one of his pencils and then almost dropped it as a sharp cramp ripped through his stomach. His hands felt sweaty. He put down the pencil and wiped his hands on his jeans. Then he started reading the first question. All around him he could hear pencils marking in the little bubbles. He bet some kids were already on the second page. As he began reading, another cramp hit him. He didn't care how many pieces of chocolate the boy in the problem had. He thought if he had a piece of chocolate now it would make him gag.

He looked at Mrs. Schraalenburgh. She was standing in front of the room watching the students.

Julio heard a moan and realized it had come from him. He didn't care if he got into a lot of trouble. He put his head down on his desk and waited for the next cramp. Almost at once Mrs. Schraalenburgh was standing above him.

"What's the problem?" she whispered. "This test isn't that hard. Come on, now. Sit up. You can do it."

Julio raised his head to look at his teacher.

She put her hand to his forehead. "Julio," she said. "You're not well. Come with me."

Julio pulled himself out of his seat and followed Mrs. Schraalenburgh to the front of the room. The pain in his gut had gotten so bad that he could hardly stand upright. All around him, Julio's classmates were looking up, puzzled.

"Go to the nurse's office and let her look at you,"

said Mrs. Schraalenburgh. She put her hand to Julio's forehead again. "I think you have a fever."

It was twelve minutes after ten when Julio reached the nurse's office. And it was fifteen minutes after ten when the nurse picked up her telephone. After that Julio lost track of the time because so many things happened. An ambulance came and he was placed on a stretcher. It was like being in a TV movie, except he felt so awful he couldn't appreciate the drama of it all. He heard the siren on the ambulance and he vaguely remembered arriving at the hospital. After that he couldn't remember anything.

It was twenty after seven when Julio opened his eyes.

"How are you feeling?" a voice asked him. It was his mother.

"Where am I?" Julio asked, feeling confused and groggy and thirsty all at once.

"You're in the hospital, man," said another voice. It was Nelson. "Hey, when you want to get out of taking a test, you don't fool around, do you?"

"What did I do?" asked Julio. He couldn't remember anything.

"You got appendicitis, that's what you did," said Ramon.

"I do?" asked Julio, surprised.

"Not anymore," said his mother, stroking his arm. He suddenly noticed his arm was attached to a tube, which was attached to a bottle hanging on a pole by the bed he was in.

"Your appendix was removed. But now I know why you didn't want to eat any breakfast. And there I was thinking it was because you were so nervous about that exam you were supposed to take."

"I was nervous," said Julio. "And I guess I still am, because I'll still have to take it, won't I?"

"One thing at a time," said his mother. "First you have to come home and get better. Then we'll worry about the exam. Mrs. Schraalenburgh said it won't be a problem for you to have a makeup."

"When did she say that?" asked Julio.

"A little while ago, when she came to see how you were doing."

"Mrs. Schraalenburgh came here?" Julio asked with surprise.

"Yeah. They wouldn't let her in the room, though," said Nelson. "'Only family till tomorrow,' the nurse said. But Mom spoke with her out in the waiting area."

"No kidding," said Julio. He didn't know what was more surprising, that he was in the hospital recovering from an operation or that his teacher had cared enough to come to check on him. It was even more surprising than seeing her at the ice-skating rink.

"She's a nice lady," said Mrs. Sanchez. "And she had lots of good things to say about you, too."

"Me? She said good things about me?" asked Julio.

"Don't be so amazed," said Ramon. "You're a great kid."

Before Ramon or Mrs. Sanchez could say anything more, a nurse walked into the room. "I'm sorry. You'll have to leave. Visiting hours are over," she said. "And I have to check out this young man with a couple of tests."

Julio looked at a clock on the wall of the hospital room. It was eight o'clock. It seemed as if there were tests all day and all night, wherever he went. Then he noticed that he was wearing a cotton gown that must belong to the hospital. He didn't remember taking off his clothing or putting this on. He must have been unconscious when that had happened. Suddenly he remembered something: what had the nurse thought when she saw all his underwear was on inside out?

11 · Visitors and Jelly Beans

"**O**h, you lucky stiff," said Lucas Cott the next day when he came to see Julio in the hospital. Lucas hardly looked at Julio as he spoke. He hadn't been in a hospital since he was born and was curious to check it out.

"What's this?" Lucas asked, pushing a button attached to a cord on Julio's bed.

"Uh-oh," said Julio. Lucas had pushed the button to summon a nurse. "What's so lucky about being sick?" he asked his classmate.

"Well, in the first place," said Lucas, sitting on the edge of the bed, "this place looks kind of interesting. Wow. Where did you get that?" he asked, noticing a huge jar of jelly beans on the night stand. "Lucky stiff," he repeated, licking his lips.

"My brothers," Julio answered. "Help yourself. I don't have any appetite for them yet."

Lucas immediately opened the jar and took a handful of candy. Then he discovered that he couldn't get his stuffed fist out of the jar. He released the jelly beans and poured some out of the jar and into his lap.

"Is there a problem here?" a voice called out, startling both Julio and Lucas. It was one of the nurses.

"Oh, no, I got special permission to come and see Julio. He's my best friend," said Lucas, jumping off of the bed and spilling the jelly beans all over the floor.

"Did you ring for me?"

"No," said Julio. "He . . ." And then, not wanting to get Lucas, who had just called him his "best friend," in trouble, he said, "I accidentally pushed the button. But I'm fine. Do you know when I'm going home?"

"The doctor will be in shortly to look at you. But I suspect he's going to want to keep you here at least one more night. You're a lucky young man. Your appendix almost perforated, you know."

"What's *perforated?*" asked Julio, looking worried. That was never on any of his vocabulary lists.

"Burst," the nurse said. "But it didn't, so you're fine."

Then the nurse looked down at the floor. "You pick up every single one of those, do you hear?" she said to Lucas, who was already picking up jelly beans and stuffing them into his mouth as fast as possible.

"Yes," he mumbled as well as he could with a mouthful of candy.

"And stop eating them," the nurse scolded. "You should never eat anything that's fallen on the floor until you wash it. Don't you know floors are dirty?"

"Nobody washes jelly beans," said Lucas, swallowing the candy in his mouth and standing up. "Besides, isn't everything in a hospital sterilized clean?"

"The surgeons' instruments are sterilized, yes, but the floor is not," the nurse said, turning on her heels. As she did so, she stepped on one of the jelly beans that Lucas had missed. "Now you know why there was a big discussion about whether or not little children should be permitted to visit the hospital," she said.

"I'm not little," Lucas retorted, defending himself and sounding a lot like one of his younger brothers. "I'm almost in fifth grade, and spilling the jelly beans was an accident. Accidents happen. Even an adult could spill them."

The nurse didn't bother to answer. She bent down and removed the candy stuck to her white oxford and threw it into the wastebasket in the corner of the room. Then she walked out.

"Still think I'm so lucky?" asked Julio with a grin.

"Well, you did get out of taking part one of the test yesterday. That was pretty good."

"Yeah," agreed Julio. "And if I stay in the hospital another night, then I guess I'll miss the next part of the test tomorrow, too. But my brother said I'll have to take makeup tests. A *makeup* test sounds dumb. Like it's about putting on lipstick or something."

"I know," said Lucas. "I asked Mrs. Schraalenburgh about it. And that's what she told me. Maybe I should have brought you one of my mother's old eyebrow pencils. But look what I did bring you as a present." From his pocket Lucas fished out a piece of paper that had been folded several times. He opened it and showed it to Julio. "These are the questions that I remembered from the test, and I asked some of the other kids to help me. I only asked smart kids like Cricket and Zoe, so I'm pretty sure these answers are the right ones."

"Cricket was willing to give the answers to me?" asked Julio with surprise. It didn't sound like her at all.

"Well, she didn't give me any answers after she figured out what I was doing with them. But before that, when the test was over and we were just sitting around and talking and guessing what we'd written that had been right and what had been wrong, I got a few from her."

"Thanks a lot," said Julio, studying the paper. "What does this mean?" he asked, pointing to a list of letters: *a c c b a a d a b.* "I thought you wrote down the questions for me."

"That would take up too much room," explained Lucas. "I'm pretty sure I remembered the questions in order and those are the answers. All you have to do is memorize the letters."

"*A c c b a a d a b* . . . it's going to be pretty hard. It doesn't make any sense at all," Julio complained. "Besides, I don't think I should use this. It sounds like cheating to me. It wouldn't be right."

"Well, I thought you'd want to have the answers," said Lucas, picking all the red jelly beans out of the jar, one at a time. "Make it like a song and sing it to yourself. *A c c b a a d a b* . . . Use a melody like 'Twinkle, Twinkle, Little Star.' It will be a piece of cake," he assured Julio as he continued munching on jelly beans.

"Why, hello Lucas," a voice called out. Julio turned his head and saw that Mrs. Schraalenburgh had walked in. Lucas grabbed for the sheet of paper and crunched it up in his hand.

"Hi, Mrs. Schraalenburgh," he said. "Do you like jelly beans?"

"Oh, you poor, poor boy," said Mrs. Schraalenburgh, coming over and kissing Julio on the forehead. Julio blushed with embarrassment. Who ever heard of a teacher doing a thing like that? He hoped he could count on his best friend to not spread the word to their classmates.

Lucas stuffed the crumpled paper under the blanket on Julio's bed. "I think I better go now," he said. "My mother is going to pick me up downstairs. I got her to drop me off here while she was doing some errands. See you soon," he told Julio.

"I'll see you tomorrow," Mrs. Schraalenburgh told Lucas.

The teacher sat down on a chair near the bed. "You poor, poor boy," she told Julio again. "Imagine trying to take that test while you were suffering from appendicitis."

"Yeah," said Julio. "I felt crummy. I thought it was because I was so nervous. I didn't know that there was something really wrong with my stomach."

"Well, when you take the makeup tests, you'll be feeling much better. We'll give you a few weeks until you're really fine and then set the dates for the new tests."

Julio's hand felt for the paper that Lucas had stuck under the cover. He didn't want his teacher to see it, but there was no way he'd memorize those letters. No matter what Lucas thought, Julio felt it would be dishonest.

"Of course, the test you take won't be exactly the same one that your classmates had," Mrs. Schraalenburgh explained.

"It won't?" asked Julio.

"Now, don't worry. It won't be one bit harder. But just as we had all those practice tests in class with different problems, the makeup test will be composed of similar but different problems. You'll do just fine. Especially since you'll be feeling so much better."

"Right," said Julio. Now he wouldn't have to worry about offending Lucas if he threw the paper in the garbage. It wouldn't do him any good at all. It contained the answers to the wrong test. "Do teachers eat jelly beans?" he asked Mrs. Schraalenburgh. "Help yourself if you do."

"Teachers are just like other people," Mrs. Schraalenburgh replied. "Some like candy and some don't. Personally, I do." She put her hand in the jar and removed a couple of the black licorice jelly beans for herself.

12 · An Unexpected Vacation

Even though Julio went home from the hospital the next day, the doctor recommended that he stay out of school for a week.

"It's best if he takes it easy. Call me if he develops a temperature or has any serious discomfort," he told Mrs. Sanchez.

"It's a good thing I got a car," said Ramon as Julio

117

climbed inside. "How would you have gotten home without Flora and me?"

"Somehow we did manage before," Mrs. Sanchez reminded her oldest son. "Remember buses?" she asked him. "Remember walking?"

"Yeah, well sure. But you can't walk home from a hospital after an operation."

"I feel fine," Julio insisted. Still, he was glad to ride home in his brother's car and he was glad to have a bonus week of unexpected vacation.

But with everyone, including his brothers, off in school, the days were long. He read the two paperback books that Mrs. Schraalenburgh had brought him at the hospital and kept up with the homework that was sent home. In addition, he watched television with his grandmother, and he helped around the house. Mrs. Sanchez suggested that he take a walk each day with his grandmother if the weather was good.

"You both need some exercise and fresh air," Mrs. Sanchez said. "Especially Abuela. She sits in front of the TV for hours and hours. It's not good for her, but because of her poor English I can't get her to join the senior center."

"Maybe we could find a special class for her so she could learn more English," Julio suggested.

"Don't think I didn't consider that myself," his mother said. "But at her age, she's not comfortable in a room full of younger people. She went once a few years ago and then refused to return."

"What about us? Ramon and Nelson and me? We're younger people. You too," he added quickly.

"It's not the same thing," said Mrs. Sanchez. "I guess she learns a little from her TV shows. At least I hope so."

Julio decided to spend some time each day teaching his grandmother English. He knew she'd never master spelling, but at least he could teach her new words and maybe even get her to read a bit. He took out his notebook from school with all the vocabulary words. He read them aloud and explained what they meant. For the first time, he looked at each word carefully. He discovered that *hurricane* and *island* were among the words. He remembered that they'd been on one of the practice tests that Mrs. Schraalenburgh had given her class. Boy, had he been dumb. Mrs. Schraalenburgh had been feeding her students answers and he hadn't even noticed. So even after his grandmother said all these new words were hurting her brain, Julio continued reviewing his vocabulary lists. There were lots of tricky words: *grateful, freezing, investigate, versatility, vehicle*. No wonder his grandmother got a headache from it all. English was a really hard language. But at least he had a head start. He knew how to speak the language and he could figure out lots of meanings from the context.

After lunch Julio remembered that he had promised to take his grandmother for a walk. Walking was not one of his grandmother's favorite activities. But she was proud to hold her grandson's arm. They walked slowly.

"There is no rush," his grandmother told him in Spanish. "Because we're not going anyplace. So we can go there slowly."

"Let's go to the supermarket," Julio suggested. "If

you have some money with you, I'll buy food and fix supper tonight all by myself."

"Oh, my," his grandmother joked. "Then it will be my turn to go to the hospital."

Nevertheless, they went to the supermarket. They walked up and down the aisles.

Julio's grandmother opened her purse. "I have ten dollars and twenty-seven cents," she said, counting the bills and adding up the coins. "Let's buy some steak for tonight while my old teeth are still strong enough to chew."

They walked over to the meat counter. Julio read the list of prices. There were several types of steak, but if he bought enough for five people of even the cheapest cut of meat, he realized he wouldn't have enough money. And besides, you couldn't have a meal of just steak. He needed to buy some vegetables to go with it.

"Sorry, Abuela," Julio said. "Keep brushing your teeth, and we'll ask Mama to buy steak after she gets paid."

At the fish counter, Julio discovered that there

was a big sale on fresh catfish, preseasoned with cajun spices. "Just put it in the oven and it's ready to eat," a sign read above the fish counter. Julio couldn't remember if he'd ever had catfish before. He didn't think so. But he was intrigued by the name. He didn't know what cajun spices were, but he decided to take a chance.

"I could cook that," said Julio to his grandmother. "It sounds easy. And it's only two ninety-nine a pound. Two pounds would be enough, and there'll be money left over for vegetables and potatoes."

"We have potatoes at home," his grandmother told him. "Your mother bought a ten-pound bag when she went shopping last week."

"Great," said Julio, wondering how many potatoes were in a ten-pound sack. "Then all we need to get are the vegetables."

So they put the fish in a shopping wagon and went to look at the vegetables to go with it. Julio weighed out a pound and a half of fresh string beans. They were $1.29 a pound, so it came to just under two dollars. There was still a little money left, and Julio thought it would be fun to make dessert, too. But he remembered that his grandmother couldn't have any sugar these days. He found a sugar-free gelatin in the dessert aisle. Julio picked out two boxes of blueberry-flavored mix and then led his grandmother over to the fruit section, where he bought a couple of bananas to slice into the mix. The gelatin was fifty-nine cents a box, and coincidentally the bananas cost the exact same amount per pound.

"Won't everyone be surprised?" Julio asked, beaming with delight at their purchases as his grandmother counted out the money to pay for everything. The total was $9.81, so there was even a little change left over—forty-six cents to be exact. It suddenly occurred to Julio that grocery shopping at the supermarket was a little bit like doing one of those practice math exams at school. Too bad forty-six cents wasn't enough for a giant bottle of soda, he thought.

At suppertime the preseasoned fish was spicy and everyone loved it. Julio had made baked potatoes to go with the string beans. He had allowed enough time so the potatoes were cooked perfectly, unlike a previous time when he had prepared a meal and they were still half raw when the meat was ready. As for the string beans, they were string beans, nothing new there. It was the dessert that turned out to be a surprise. It had been a bit startling to Julio when he had prepared it. It was a bright blue color that was not at all the color of blueberries. Nevertheless, it looked familiar. Did he once have a shirt that shade? It wasn't until Nelson blurted out, "What's this? A bowl of toilet cleaner?" that Julio realized where he'd seen that color before. With that thought in mind, it was hard for anyone to have an appetite for the gelatin. But it was Julio's grandmother who saved the situation.

"Turn out the lights and put a candle on the table," she instructed Julio. When you couldn't see what you were eating, it didn't taste so bad after all.

"Bravo, Julio! This was a great meal," complimented Mrs. Sanchez.

13 · The Makeup Test

"**B**ravo, Julio. Welcome back to school," said Mrs. Schraalenburgh on the following Monday morning when he returned to his classroom.

Julio smiled. He looked around the room at his classmates. How lucky they all were to have those standardized tests behind them. He wondered when Mrs. Schraalenburgh was going to give him the makeup tests. Maybe, he thought, if he was very, very lucky, she'd forget.

But of course, he wasn't and she didn't. As he was leaving the room at dismissal time that day, Mrs. Schraalenburgh told Julio that the following Monday he would take the language arts makeup test. "Two students from other fourth-grade classes missed the test as well. They both were absent with bronchitis. So the three of you will take the test together in the school library. And I've arranged for you to take the math section of the exam a week from Wednesday."

"Maybe I'll get sick again," said Julio. "I know the doctor said I could never, ever get appendicitis again, but since the last test made that happen to me, I think I might get something else when I take the makeup test. Maybe I'll get bronchitis like those other kids did."

"Don't be silly," said Mrs. Schraalenburgh. "You're a healthy boy. It's just a coincidence that you came down with appendicitis on the day the state sched-uled those standardized tests. The appendicitis was just something waiting to happen. It could have occurred during the winter when we were all ice-skating. Or it could have happened during the summer vacation."

"I might get sick again," insisted Julio, looking worried.

"Now don't talk yourself into it," said his teacher. "You'll be fine and you'll do fine too." She paused a moment. "Are you in a rush to get home? Or can you stay for a couple of minutes?"

Julio wondered what his teacher wanted. Was she going to give him another practice test right now?

"I can stay," he told her.

"Good, then come sit down and let me talk to you," Mrs. Schraalenburgh said. "I've said this before actually, but I don't think it registered with you. These state tests are given to check that the teachers are doing their jobs. They are testing me just as much as they are testing you. And if you don't do well, it means I haven't done what I'm paid to do. Teach."

"You're a good teacher," Julio said. "Everyone says

you're the best fourth-grade teacher in the school. Even Cricket says we're lucky to be in this class," he added.

"Well, that's nice to hear from you," said Mrs. Schraalenburgh, smiling. "But the state needs more than personal comments from my students to make its assessment. And that's why you have to take the tests next week. It's nothing to work yourself up about. Do you understand?"

"If I don't do well, will I have to repeat fourth grade?" asked Julio.

"Absolutely not," his teacher said. "I've enjoyed having you in my class, but you're much too smart to sit through fourth grade another time."

"I am?" asked Julio, surprised.

"You certainly are," said Mrs. Schraalenburgh. "Now promise me you won't worry any more about the tests. All right?"

"Yes, but when I grow up, I'm never going to take another test again," Julio vowed.

"That's easy to say, but I'm afraid it's not at all true," said Mrs. Schraalenburgh. "Life is full of tests for us at all ages, and you'll discover that you'll never be rid of them."

Julio nodded. "I forgot," he admitted to his teacher. "My brother is older than me. He just took his road test to get a driver's license. And my grandmother had to go and take tests from her doctor."

"Life is full of tests," Mrs. Schraalenburgh repeated. "Think about it: in sports they do drug testing to be sure that the players don't cheat by taking medications that will enhance their abilities; when someone drives erratically, the police often stop them and test whether or not they are drunk because drunk drivers are very dangerous on the road; there are medical tests like mammograms and sonograms, biopsies, and blood tests—all tests to check on your health. Tests help us learn the truth. And the truth is important. The nurse gives eye tests every year. That tells us the truth about your vision. Looking at your face and seeing your two brown eyes would never tell me how well you can see with those eyes." Mrs. Schraalenburgh stopped. "Do I make my point?" she asked.

Julio nodded. Tests might not always be the most pleasant thing to do, but he was beginning to understand that they were important and necessary.

"Good, then stop worrying," said Mrs. Schraalenburgh. "Go home, play with your friends, eat your supper, do your homework. And next week you'll take the statewide exams just as all your classmates already did. They all survived and so will you."

The following Monday, the three *itis* students, as Julio had begun calling the two who had bronchitis and himself, sat at three empty tables in the school library. "You know the procedure," said Mrs. Moorehead, the librarian. "But let me remind you. There is to be no talking. When I say 'Pencils down,' you are to stop writing. Are there any questions before we start?"

The three kids shook their heads.

"Good," said Mrs. Moorehead. "You may open your booklet and begin."

Julio began. Some of the answers he knew easily. He smiled to himself when he recognized words like *huricane* and *islend*. He knew they were spelled incorrectly. Some of the words were too tricky for him, however. He guessed a few of them, but some he was pretty sure he got right.

When Mrs. Moorehead said, "Pencils down," he promptly obeyed. He was done. The test was over. Mrs. Moorehead picked up the three test booklets and smiled at the students.

"You may return to your classrooms now," she told them.

Julio walked across the library and out the door. It felt so good to be finished with at least one part of the test after all those weeks of worrying about it that, although he knew it was forbidden, he made a few leaps down the hallway. He almost let out a whoop of relief as well, but at the last moment he remembered where he was. There might not be any warning signs asking for silence on the classroom doors, but he knew he shouldn't shout out. So he kept his mouth shut and continued down the hallway quietly, as if there were a test in progress. Of course, he still had the math test ahead of him, but he was no longer worried about it. He might not do as well as Cricket or Lucas, but he'd do the best he could. That's all that was expected of him. When he reached the door of his fourth-grade classroom, he walked inside. No one could tell that once again his underwear was on inside out.